Dear Parent:
Your child's love of reading starts here!

Every child learns to read in a different way and at his or her own speed. Some go back and forth between reading levels and read favorite books again and again. Others read through each level in order. You can help your young reader improve and become more confident by encouraging his or her own interests and abilities. From books your child reads with you to the first books he or she reads alone, there are I Can Read Books for every stage of reading:

SHARED READING
Basic language, word repetition, and whimsical illustrations, ideal for sharing with your emergent reader

BEGINNING READING
Short sentences, familiar words, and simple concepts for children eager to read on their own

READING WITH HELP
Engaging stories, longer sentences, and language play for developing readers

READING ALONE
Complex plots, challenging vocabulary, and high-interest topics for the independent reader

I Can Read Books have introduced children to the joy of reading since 1957. Featuring award-winning authors and illustrators and a fabulous cast of beloved characters, I Can Read Books set the standard for beginning readers.

A lifetime of discovery begins with the magical words **"I Can Read!"**

Visit www.icanread.com for information
on enriching your child's reading experience.

Pinkalicious®
Happy Birthday!

To YOU, on your birthday!
—V.K.

The author gratefully acknowledges
the artistic and editorial contributions of
Daniel Griffo and Jacqueline Resnick.

I Can Read® and I Can Read Book® are trademarks of HarperCollins Publishers.

Pinkalicious: Happy Birthday!
Copyright © 2021 by VBK, Co.

PINKALICIOUS and all related logos and characters are trademarks of Victoria Kann. Used with permission.

Based on the HarperCollins book *Pinkalicious* written by
Victoria Kann and Elizabeth Kann, illustrated by Victoria Kann
All rights reserved. Printed in the United States of America.
No part of this book may be used or reproduced in any manner whatsoever without
written permission except in the case of brief quotations embodied in critical articles and reviews.
For information address HarperCollins Children's Books, a division of HarperCollins Publishers,
195 Broadway, New York, NY 10007.
www.icanread.com

Library of Congress Control Number: 2020938947
ISBN 978-0-06-284054-7 (trade bdg.)—ISBN 978-0-06-284053-0 (pbk.)

21 22 23 24 25 LSCC 10 9 8 7 6 5 4 3 2 1
❖
First Edition

I Can Read!

BEGINNING 1 READING

Pinkalicious®
Happy Birthday!

by Victoria Kann

HARPER
An Imprint of HarperCollins Publishers

"Today is my birthday!
I can't wait for everyone
to get here so my party can start!"
I said to my brother, Peter.

HAPPY BIRTHDAY,
Pinkalicious!

"The baker is bringing
the most pinkatastic, pinkamazing,
pinkabeautiful cake ever," I said.
"I want the first bite!" said Peter.
"When it's your birthday,
you get to eat the first piece,"
said Daddy.

"This chair could use
some pink party pizzazz," I said.
"I can add balloons
to your birthday throne to make it
more pinkafestive," said Peter.
He tied balloons to the chair.
"More?" Peter asked.
"Yes, MORE!" I said.
"More, more, more!"

"Uh-oh," said Peter.

"Your throne is floating!"

"Oh no." I gasped.

"The balloons are lifting

me up in the air!"

12

"Pinkalicious, what are you doing?"
asked Mommy.

"Come back, Pinkalicious!"
yelled Daddy.

"I don't know how!" I said.

I rose above the treetops.

I could see my friends below,

coming to my party.

"Helloooo!" I called to them.

"What are you doing?" asked Molly.

"I didn't get to fly on my birthday,"
Alison said.

The wind blew me right past them
before I could answer.

I floated over Pinkville.

"Hey, Pinkalicious,"

said Mr. Swizzle.

"Happy birthday!"

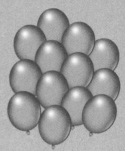

I floated over a soccer game.

"Go, Pinksters!" I yelled.

"HAPPY BIRTHDAY, Pinkalicious!"
the team yelled back.

"Hello, birthday girl!"
the baker called up to me.
She had the prettiest
cake I'd ever seen.

"I have to get home so Peter doesn't
eat the first slice!" I said.

I looked down. I was way up high.

Suddenly the air grew colder.

The wind picked up speed.

It blew me even farther from home.

When the wind slowed down,

I was so far away

that I couldn't even see my house!

"How will I get back

to my party now?" I gasped.

There was another gust of wind.

I was flying with the birds!

"Can you help me get home?"

I asked.

"Tweet, tweet," said the birds.

22

They flew even closer to me.

I heard a strange POP POP!

"Uh-oh," I said.

Their beaks had punctured

a couple of my balloons by mistake!

My chair spun and twirled

as the balloons lost air.

I sank a little lower.

When I finally stopped spinning,

I could see my house!

The baker was delivering my cake.

Peter grabbed a fork.

"Cake time!" I heard him say.

A breeze pushed me toward my house.

"Drop that fork!" I yelled.

Everyone turned.

"Look, it's Pinkalicious!" Molly said.

"Just in time!" said Rose.

"Thank goodness," Mommy said.

"How do we get you down?"

asked Daddy.

I thought about how my chair

had sunk after the balloons popped.

"I have an idea," I said.

I untied a balloon.

I sank lower in the sky.

"It's working!" Alison said.

I untied the balloons one by one.

Everyone sang as I floated down.

"Happy birthday to you,

happy birthday to you,

happy birthday, dear Pinkalicious,

happy birthday to you!"

I blew out my candle,

but I couldn't come up with a wish!

"You'll think of one," Daddy said.

Mommy cut the first slice of cake.

I was about to take a bite

when I saw Peter's face.

"Okay, okay, Peter," I said.

"You can have the first piece."

"No, you eat it," Peter said.

"It's your birthday, after all."

"How about if we share?" I said.

We both took a bite.

"This cake tastes as pinkayummy
as it looks!" I said.

Suddenly I knew
the perfect wish.
"I wish every birthday
could be as PINKAFUN
as this one!" I said.